The BLACK PEARL PONIES series:

1: Red Star

2: Wildflower

3: Miss Molly

4: Stormcloud

5: Snickers

6: Ghost Horse

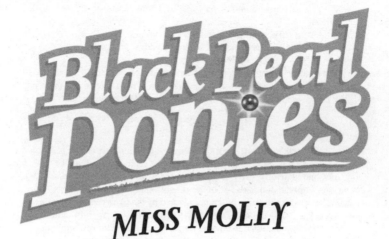

MISS MOLLY

JENNY OLDFIELD

Illustrated by
JOHN GREEN

Hodder
Children's
Books

A division of Hachette Children's Books

First published in Great Britain in 2011
by Hodder Children's Books

2

A Catalogue record for this book is available from the British Library

ISBN 978 0 340 99894 6

Printed and bound in the UK by
CPI Group (UK) Ltd, Croydon, CR0 4YY

The paper and board used in this paperback by
Hodder Children's Books are natural recyclable products made from wood
grown in sustainable forests. The manufacturing processes conform to the
environmental regulations of the country of origin.

Hodder Children's Books
A division of Hachette Children's Books
338 Euston Road, London NW1 3BH
An Hachette UK company
www.hachette.co.uk

*Once more with thanks to the Foster family
and all my friends at Lost Valley Ranch, and this
time with special thanks to Katie Foster, horse
trainer and all-round equine expert.*

CHAPTER ONE

'This has to be a secret!' The visitor to Black Pearl Ranch drew Keira to one side. 'Sable doesn't know anything about Miss Molly – it's going to be her big birthday surprise!'

Keira nodded. 'I promise I won't tell her.'

'My daughter will be ten years old at the end of the month,' Mrs Hearne went on. 'I finally persuaded her dad to buy her a pony. We need Miss Molly to be fully trained and ready by then.'

'My dad will do a good job,' Keira told her. She had one eye on the trailer parked in the yard, eager to get her first sight of the new arrival.

'We chose him because we heard he's the best trainer in the county.' Caroline Hearne sounded serious and a little worried. 'Sable has never been around horses, so we want to be sure that Miss Molly is totally reliable. We don't want a pony that spooks easily or one that has a nasty temper.'

Keira nodded but she was hardly listening. Across the yard she saw her dad walk to the back of the Hearnes' trailer and open the door. Any moment now Miss Molly would be stepping down the ramp.

'Hey, Keira, open the barn door!' Her dad, Jacob, called. 'I plan to lead Miss Molly out of the trailer right into her stall.'

'It's OK – I've got it!' Suddenly Keira's big sister, Brooke, appeared. She ran to the barn and opened the door. 'Ready, Dad!'

'We're giving your father two weeks to train her to perfection,' Mrs Hearne went on. 'Do you think he can do it?'

'Sure.' Keira itched to get away. She heard Miss Molly give a couple of nervous snorts as her dad untied her and turned her around inside the trailer ready for unloading. 'Mrs Hearne, I've got to go now – Dad might need my help.'

'That's OK, Keira – I'll talk Caroline through what happens over the next couple of weeks.' Luckily Keira's mom, Allyson, had come out of the house and let her off the hook. 'Exactly how old is Miss Molly?' she asked as Keira scooted off. 'And has she ever had a saddle on her back, or are we starting from scratch here?'

'Easy now.' Jacob's voice was gentle as he led Miss

Molly out of the trailer into the daylight.

Keira stood at the barn door next to Brooke when she got her first sight of the little sorrel pony, and it took her breath away.

Miss Molly was a beautiful, shiny, nut-brown colour from head to toe, except for the pure white flash running the length of her nose. Her mane was thick and silky; her tail almost brushed the ground. And her face – well, Keira thought her face was the prettiest she'd ever seen.

'Oh, so cute!' Brooke gasped.

'Those eyes!' Keira sighed. Miss Molly's eyes were big and deep brown. Her nose was curved beautifully, her ears pricked and pointing straight ahead.

'Wait for me!' A man's voice broke the awed silence. It was Mr Hearne, jumping down from the cab of the trailer. He slammed the door, making Miss Molly jump and leap sideways off the ramp. For a moment it looked as though she might break free.

'Steady – whoa!' Jacob took the strain on the end of the lead rope. He let the pony find her footing on the gravel surface then waited for her to settle before he began to lead her across the yard with Mr Hearne striding after them.

'She moves like a dream!' Like Keira, Brooke

had fallen in love at first sight. 'So smooth, so easy.'

'And she carries her head real high. See how she arches her neck!'

'Like a thoroughbred,' Brooke murmured.

The girls stood aside as their dad and Miss Molly reached the door.

'That's right, stand back – don't go crowding her or fooling around,' Martin Hearne told them. She's had a rough ride over from the other side of Sheriton and that dirt track of yours needs some work, Lucas.'

'It's a little rough in parts,' Jacob agreed. It now seemed he was in no hurry to lead Miss Molly into her stall. Instead he decided to give her time to get accustomed to her new surroundings – the yard and corral, the clear creek running through the meadow beyond the barn, the small knot of Black Pearl horses and ponies gathered at the split-rail fence. 'My neighbour, Tom Walters, has offered to lend me his grader to smooth out the worst of the ridges, but it's one of those jobs that doesn't ever quite make it to the top of my list, I guess.'

'The sooner the better,' Hearne grumbled. He was a small man with a balding head, wearing a cream sweatshirt and jeans that hadn't seen much hard work to judge by their neatly ironed creases. 'The bumps in that road threw my pony all over the place in the back of my trailer. She could have broken a leg.'

'She's a pretty little thing.' Jacob sidestepped the argument that was building up and instead ran his expert eye over Miss Molly's good, deep chest and strong withers. 'Three years old, you say?'

Martin Hearne nodded. 'Pure Quarter Horse. She has the right papers; comes from good breeding stock. And I paid a high price, I can tell you.'

'Three is a little late to start the basic training,' Jacob noted. 'But she's been fed and kept right by the look of things.'

'You can do a good job with her?' Hearne fixed his new horse trainer with a searching look. 'You won't let me down?'

'I'll sure try not to,' Keira's dad replied while Keira frowned at Brooke. The girls didn't like Mr Hearne's tone of voice. Didn't he know that no one in Sheriton County knew as much about training and bringing on young ponies as their brilliant dad?

'And you girls realise that this pony is a big secret

– that my daughter, Sable, doesn't know a thing about it?' Hearne turned towards them without softening his voice. 'My wife told you that this is a surprise?'

'I made it totally clear,' Caroline Hearne said, arriving at the barn door with Allyson. 'If – *when* you girls bump into Sable at school next week, you don't breathe a word.'

'Got it,' Keira muttered abruptly. Her mom shot her a warning glance and Keira was glad when Brooke stepped in.

'We won't say a thing, Mrs Hearne,' Brooke said, super-polite. 'Sable is going to have the best surprise in the world when her birthday comes around!'

'Red Star, you'll never believe how beautiful she is!' The fussy, bad-tempered Hearnes had finally driven their trailer back along the Lucases' rough dirt track and Keira was riding her own pony bareback from the meadow into the corral. 'I mean, really and truly she's a drop-dead gorgeous sorrel with a white flash and the prettiest face ...'

Red Star picked up his rider's excitement and broke into a trot towards the gate. Behind them the sun was sinking fast behind the jagged peaks of Black Pearl Mountains.

'Whoa there!' Keira laughed as she bent forward to release the gate catch. 'Miss Molly isn't going anywhere. She's bedded down nice and cosy in the stall next to yours. You have all night to get acquainted!'

Red Star shook his head and tossed his mane. It was as if he understood. *Let me into that barn!* he seemed to say.

Red Star and Keira had been partners from day one. In fact they'd been born on the same day in May ten years earlier, soon after the Lucas family had moved out of the city to live at Black Pearl Ranch. They'd grown up together – Keira the toddler with her big grey eyes and mop of red-blonde hair, Red Star, the gangling, strawberry-roan foal. They'd grown tall together in the meadows of the steep-sided valley, paddled side by side in the clear creek and explored the forest trails past Dolphin Rock out towards Sharman Lake. 'You'll never separate those two,' Allyson would tell visitors when they watched Keira and Red Star ride out together. 'They're joined at the hip – always were, always will be.'

Now Keira slid back the gate catch and let her pony push the gate open with his broad chest. He trotted across the yard, straight through the open barn door.

'Who-o-oa!' Jacob was next to the grain store, scooping feed into a barrow. He had to step quickly to one side as Red Star and Keira barged past.

'Sorry, Dad. I've been telling him about Miss Molly. He can't wait to meet her!'

'Yeah, he speaks fluent English as well as his native Horse!' Jacob grinned.

'He does!' Keira slipped from her pony's back

and let him walk right on.

He stepped down the aisle as if he owned the place – head up, snickering a greeting to Brooke's pony, Annie, in her stall to the right and stopping briefly to nuzzle the noses of the two brood mares, Ruby and Willow.

'He sure is a character!' Jacob laughed. 'You reckon he and Miss Molly will get along?'

'I already told him how pretty she is,' Keira explained.

'But a little young for Red Star, don't you think?'

'Keira shrugged. 'Three isn't so young.'

'Four, actually,' her dad corrected. 'Her papers say three, but I checked her mouth and she's more like four going on five.'

'See!' Miss Molly was almost five to Red Star's

ten. 'Perfect. Look at him now – playing hard to get!'

As they chatted, Red Star had gone right up to the visitor's stall, taken one swift glance at the pretty sorrel, then turned his attention to a hay net hanging from a hook at the door to his own stall. He took a large mouthful and began to chew.

Keira ran down the aisle to join him. 'Hey!' she protested. 'Show some manners – say hi properly.'

Red Star sighed and chewed. *In my own good time.* Munch-munch.

Meanwhile, Miss Molly looked curiously over her stall door. She stared at Red Star and gave him a low whinny.

'Red Star, Miss Molly is saying hi!' Keira got

around the far side of her pony and leaned on him,
pushing him towards the sorrel's door. 'Miss Molly,
this is Red Star. Red Star, meet Miss Molly.'

The visitor whinnied again. Red Star ducked his
head and swerved back towards the hay net.

'What's up? Why aren't you being nice?' Keira wanted to know. 'You're usually so good with our guests.'

It took Jacob to work it out. He strode down the aisle and leaned against Miss Molly's door, reaching out to pat her neck and run his hand through her silky mane. Meanwhile, Red Star kept his back turned as he shuffled into his stall for the night. 'Not a happy fellow,' he commented.

'Why not? What's up with him?' After all Keira had said about Miss Molly, after all Red Star's earlier eagerness to get into the barn, why had he suddenly changed his mind?

Keira's pony stood in his stall, head down and deliberately ignoring them all.

'You said too much,' Jacob told Keira. 'Red Star

listened to your tone of voice. He knows you fell in

love with Miss Molly and now he's jealous!'

CHAPTER TWO

'Two weeks doesn't give us much time,' Jacob told Brooke and Keira early next morning.

He'd asked the girls to bring Miss Molly out of the barn into the corral where they brushed her down and combed her mane and tail. Now he was clipping a rope to her head collar, ready to lead her into the round pen.

'Has she ever had a saddle on before now?' Brooke wanted to know.

'I pass on that,' their dad replied, walking Miss Molly out of the corral. 'The Hearnes were a little hazy on this pony's history.'

'Yeah. Mr Hearne thought she was three years old,' Keira recalled. 'And she's actually almost five.'

'They haven't been around horses, so I guess they didn't ask the right questions when they bought her. And the documents establishing her Quarter Horse status look a little suspect. Who knows? Anyhow, we start right at the beginning with this little lady, just working on join-up until she gets to know us.'

Keira ran ahead to open the gate. She felt excited this cold, bright Sunday morning, knowing they had the whole day ahead of them to start Miss Molly's training.

'How was Red Star when you took him out to the meadow this morning? Was he still giving you a hard time?' As he began work on persuading the sorrel to take instructions from him in the round pen, Jacob chatted easily. He unclipped the lead rope and let Miss Molly explore.

'Still jealous,' Keira admitted. 'But I promised I'd ride him out along the trail after I'd finished here. That'll put him in a better mood.'

'Annie and I will come with you,' Brooke

offered. 'Let's ride out to the Three Horseshoes to see Reed.'

'Deal,' Keira agreed, eagerly tuning into the activity in the pen.

She loved to watch this – a pony's first session with her dad.

First off, Jacob would take his coiled rope from the fence post and flick it out straight along the ground, coming up just close enough to the pony's heels to make her break into a trot away from the end of the rope. Then he would keep working at the rope, snaking it along the ground, keeping the untrained pony moving around the outer rim of the pen.

'Nice work!' Brooke called as she sat on the fence. Miss Molly was trotting smoothly, one ear

flicked back, paying full attention to the pesky rope.

'So beautiful!' Keira sighed. You could take a full-colour, high-definition picture of the little sorrel and make a perfect pony poster for a kid's bedroom.

'Red Star, close your ears!' Brooke joked, even though he was nowhere near. They watched as gradually Miss Molly grew tired of trotting, of being driven on by Jacob's rope, so that her head went down, her pace slowed and she asked to stop.

'Good girl!' Jacob eased off on the rope. He stood in the centre of the pen, his head turned away from the pony, waiting for her to approach.

'Easy, easy!' Keira breathed, perched on the fence next to Brooke. Her dad timed it perfectly, gave exactly the right body language to allow Miss

Molly to walk up to him as if to say, *OK, what next?*
She smiled as the sorrel nuzzled Jacob's arm.
'You've got it, Miss Molly – Dad's the boss around
here!'

'Perfect join-up!' It was Allyson's voice, coming
from outside the pen. 'Nice and easy, nice and
gentle.'

Keira jumped down from the fence to join her
mom. 'Miss Molly's not just a pretty face – she's
smart too. I reckon Dad will have no problem
training her and getting her back to Sable Hearne
before her birthday.'

Allyson nodded. 'You want to come to the tack
room with me and pick out a saddle?'

Keira nodded and ran ahead. In the tack room
doorway she stopped to scoop up the ginger kitten

that had strayed on to the ranch one day last week and decided to stay. Keira had named him Popcorn. She was the one who'd been given the job of feeding him and taking care of him.

'Hey, kitty!' she murmured, cuddling him then putting him down on the pile of saddle pads near the door. 'Will Dad need a bridle for Miss Molly as well as a saddle?' she asked her mom.

'Not today. He'll want to work her in the round pen, first with a saddle pad then with the saddle on top. The bridle comes later.' Allyson went down the row of saddles all neatly stowed on strong wooden brackets along the length of the tack room. 'Too small,' she murmured 'Too heavy ... Maybe this one.'

Miaow! Popcorn rubbed up against Keira's leg,

his little
pointed tail
sticking straight
in the air.
'I hear you!'
she laughed.
'But you
already had your
breakfast.' She stooped to take a
red and black patterned pad from the pile. Then she
headed out on to the porch where she stopped to
watch Miss Molly going through the whole join-up
routine over again. Soon she heard her mom come
up close behind.

'Neat,' Allyson said, nodding her approval.

'Isn't Miss Molly adorable?' Keira's eyes

sparkled. 'Wouldn't you just die to get a birthday present like that?'

Her mom agreed. There was a long pause then she said. 'I only hope Sable Hearne knows how lucky she is.'

It was Thursday of that week before Keira saw Sable. From Monday to Wednesday Keira and Brooke were home-schooled – it was only on Thursdays and Fridays that they made the long bus trip in to Sheriton to attend the middle school there.

'Remember, not a word to Sable about Miss Molly!' their mom warned as she dropped them off at the bus stop.

Keira hated secrets. They were like elephants in

the room – always getting in your way and tripping you up. So the second she saw Sable Hearne heading down the corridor towards her, she almost broke her promise – as in, *Hey Sable, you'll never believe the birthday present your folks have bought you! A totally gorgeous sorrel mare with a white flash on her face and the thickest, silkiest mane you ever saw!*

'Hey Sable,' was what she actually said, stammering as her tongue stuck to the roof of her mouth. 'How are you doing?'

'Good.' Sable Hearne was in Keira's class but they weren't close buddies. She was the type of kid who didn't make friends easily – choosing maybe one or two people to sit with in class and rarely joining in with group sport or music activity after school. Small and skinny, dark like her mom, she was shy and couldn't seem to help coming across as stand-offish. Today she appeared annoyed that Keira had even said hello.

Keira stumbled on. 'I hear your birthday's coming up soon.' *Oops, shouldn't have mentioned the birthday!*

Sable sniffed. 'Where did you hear that?'

'Oh … er … um…'

'We ran into your mom in the grocery store.' Brooke stepped in to rescue Keira. Secretly she gave her a shove with her elbow. 'What's top of your wish list, Sable?'

'The usual,' Sable replied, still offhand. She tugged at the fringe of her woollen scarf and stared at her feet. 'Wii games, clothes maybe.'

Just then, Lisa Shaw, Sable's one and only true

friend, caught up with her. 'And?' Lisa prompted. 'Go ahead, Sable – tell Keira and Brooke what you really want!'

Sable shook her head. 'What's the point? I'm not going to get it.'

'It's a pony!' motormouth Lisa burbled on. 'Sable's mom and dad are loaded. They can easily afford to buy her a pony and build a stable and an arena in their gigantic yard. But her dad says no way, ponies are too much trouble, what with the feeding and the farrier and the vet's visits. Plus, Sable's bedroom walls may be lined with pony pictures but she's never ridden one in her entire life.'

As Lisa rambled on and Sable turned red with embarrassment, Keira and Brooke coughed and shuffled. The secret of Miss Molly weighed even heavier than they'd expected.

Then Keira spotted Mrs Taylor, their science teacher, turn the corner. 'Gotta go!' she gasped, heading for her lesson faster than usual. End of conversation, thank heavens!

For the rest of Thursday and all of Friday Keira succeeded in avoiding Sable Hearne. But she thought a lot about what Lisa had said and, on the bus home on Friday, she talked to Brooke about it.

'I reckon Sable and Miss Molly will be good together.' Keira was staring out of the window at the distant, misty mountains. 'I mean, I realise Sable doesn't know about ponies and her mom and dad seemed kind of mean, but the big thing is, she's always wanted to own her own pony and when she sees Miss Molly she'll fall in love with her the way we did, and after that everything will kind of fall into place and Miss Molly will have a good home and Sable can get lessons from Mom on how to ride and pretty soon it will all be just perfect ...'

'Whoa!' Brooke stopped her at last. 'You've been working this out, haven't you?'

Keira nodded. She turned to her big sister with a sudden, worried frown. 'I'm right, aren't I?' she whispered. 'Miss Molly is going to be OK?'

CHAPTER THREE

Next morning Keira was up with the lark, first feeding Popcorn on the tack room porch then helping her dad get ready for another training session with her favourite sorrel. This time though, instead of walking Red Star out to the meadow, she saddled him in the corral.

'Today you get to help little Miss Molly,' she explained, brushing the dirt out of his speckled, reddish-brown and white coat. 'We join her in the round pen, you and me, and we show her a few things she needs to know.'

Red Star turned his head towards the pen and saw Miss Molly ready saddled, with Jacob and Brooke standing nearby. As soon as Keira had lifted his saddle onto his back and tightened his cinch he was raring to go.

'Here we come!' Keira called. 'Open the gate, guys!'

In they went, Red Star prancing a little as he entered the round pen, head high and showing off for Miss Molly's benefit. When Keira reined him to the left and asked him to do an anti-clockwise circuit, he responded proudly, extending his trot to show how strong and athletic he was.

'OK, Keira, bring him over here,' Jacob told her. 'Stand him beside Miss Molly while Brooke gets on her back.'

'Good boy,' Keira breathed, patting his neck as he stood good as gold.

Jacob held Miss Molly's reins while Brooke eased herself into the saddle. 'See, nothing to it,' he murmured in the pony's ear. 'OK, Keira, you walk Red Star around now, and Brooke, you ask Miss Molly to follow.'

Gently Keira squeezed both legs against Red Star's sides. 'This is most likely the first time Miss Molly has ever been ridden,' she told him. 'We take it easy – no tricks, no fancy stuff.' Glancing back, she saw Brooke sitting firm in the saddle with loose reins, letting Miss Molly make her own decision to follow Red Star.

'That's good,' Jacob said quietly. 'You're all doing just fine.'

Just then a rider appeared on the Jeep trail. He was approaching fast, his brown and white Appaloosa kicking up dirt as they came. Keira peered over the top rail of the round pen and recognised their neighbour and good friend, Reed

Walters. 'Shall I go ask him to quieten down?' she asked her dad, who nodded then strode across the pen to stop Miss Molly from following.

Quickly Keira and Red Star trotted out along the trail to meet Reed and Wildflower. 'Dad's busy working,' she warned Reed. 'It's a new sorrel – never been ridden.'

Straight away Reed slowed down. 'Sorry if I broke in on something. Is it OK for me to take a look? I'll stay well back from the fence.'

'Sure. This pony is beautiful. Brooke's riding her and they're doing great.' Proudly, Keira led the way back to the round pen.

They found Jacob giving more quiet instructions to Brooke. 'Neck-rein her towards the centre. Put on a little pressure with your left leg – that's good.'

Slowly, without any force, Brooke eased Miss Molly into following her instructions. Then in the centre of the pen she tugged at the reins to bring her to a halt.

'She learns fast,' Keira whispered to Reed.

He nodded. 'Who owns her?'

'She belongs to … erm … er …' Keira stopped

herself just in time. 'Sorry, I can't tell you that.'

'Only, I reckon I've seen her before.'

'You have?' Keira's eyes widened. She would love to learn more of Miss Molly's history.

'Yeah. She's the right height and the same colouring – the white flash on her nose and all.' Reed studied Miss Molly at work in the round pen. 'How old is she?'

'Coming up for five. I know – it's kind of old to get her started. We don't understand the background to that. But Dad worked real hard to get her saddled up within a week. The new owners want her ready to go by the end of the month.'

'And she's doing OK?' Reed edged nearer to the pen for a better view. 'It's the same pony, for sure.'

'And?' Keira guessed there was more.

'She came from the Allens' place out past Elk Springs.'

'And?' Keira prompted again. Honestly, dragging information out of Reed was like getting blood from a stone.

He frowned. 'You don't know the family, but Luke Allen bought her for his youngest brother, Jay, when she was about two years old. The family kept her for a while but in the end it didn't work out.'

Now it was Keira's turn to frown. She looked anxiously through the fence rails at Brooke and her dad teaching Miss Molly to walk forward in a straight line. 'Exactly how didn't it work out?'

Reed screwed up his mouth and shrugged. 'It just didn't – that's all I know.'

CHAPTER FOUR

'Reed doesn't make mistakes.' It was Saturday lunchtime and Brooke sat opposite Keira at the kitchen table sticking up for her friend from the Three Horseshoes. 'If he says he recognises Miss Molly from the Allens' place, he's probably right.'

'How can he be?' Keira refused to believe that the previous owners could have had a problem with Miss Molly. 'This is the perfect pony we're talking about here!'

'I'm just saying,' Brooke shrugged. 'Reed knows what he's talking about.'

'Yeah, like he knew what he was talking about when he entered Wildflower into the rodeo before she was ready that time.' Keira reminded Brooke of Reed's bad mistake but regretted it straightaway. *Ouch!* Sometimes her tongue ran away with her. 'Sorry, I shouldn't have said that.'

Allyson stepped in fast. 'Apology accepted, Keira. Now let's clear away the plates and get in an hour's schoolwork before we begin our afternoon chores.'

Keira's mom gave her an English task – *Make a list of six things you wish you'd never said.*

'Aw, Mom!' Keira sighed. 'I already told Brooke I was sorry.'

Allyson stuck to her guns. 'You know how Brooke feels about her friendship with Reed, especially since he ended up in the hospital.'

'I do. But how can Reed be right about Miss Molly? No way can this be the same pony.'

'Keira!' Allyson warned. She put a pen and a pad of paper on the table in front of her. 'Make the list!'

Keira bent her head and concentrated.

Six things I wish I'd never said:

1. I wish I hadn't been mean about Reed and Wildflower in front of my sister.

2. I wish I hadn't made Red Star jealous by praising Miss Molly too much.

3. I wish

She got stuck on 3 and stared out of the window at Popcorn sitting on a fence post in the midday sun. She jumped up when she saw a black SUV drive into the yard. 'Visitors! Mom, Dad – we have visitors!'

There was no reply so Keira abandoned her

school work and ran out on to the porch in time to see Mr and Mrs Hearne step out of the vehicle.

'Hey, young lady,' Martin Hearne greeted her. He seemed in a better mood than the last time Keira had seen him. 'We dropped by to check progress on our sorrel mare.'

'She's doing great!' Spotting her dad already at work after lunch, Keira led Sable's parents across the yard to the round pen. 'Here she is. Brooke rode her for the first time this morning. That's pretty good progress for the end of week one.'

'And you didn't breathe a word to Sable about her birthday surprise?' Caroline Hearne checked.

'I swear. Shall I ask Dad if I can ride Miss Molly for you?'

Martin Hearne nodded. 'Sure. Then send him

across to talk to us, why don't you?'

Smiling, Keira carried the message to her dad. He waited until she was safely in the saddle then left the pen to chat with the Hearnes.

Keira leaned forward and spoke softly into the pony's ear. 'OK, Miss Molly, it's time to show your new owners what you can do.'

A gentle squeeze eased the sorrel into a smooth walk. Miss Molly carried Keira calmly and confidently, settling into a full circuit then listening to the quiet command to stop. 'Good girl!' Keira breathed.

'That's just the basics,' Jacob was telling the Hearnes. 'Tomorrow we start taking Miss Molly out on the trails, get her used to being in the forest, put some miles on her.'

'There's no need to do that,' Martin Hearne pointed out, almost tripping over Popcorn who had jumped down from the fence and wanted to be petted. 'Sable will only be riding this pony in an indoor arena I'm planning to have one built in our backyard.'

'Still, you said you wanted to give your girl a

bomb-proof ride,' Jacob reminded him. 'Trail riding will do that.'

'Yeah well, I guess you know your business,' Hearne said, sounding as if he didn't really mean what he said. Then, without thinking, he moved suddenly to open the gate into the round pen just at the point when Keira and Miss Molly were walking by.

'Whoa!' Keira said as the pony laid back her ears and skittered sideways. She kept her seat, gave the halt command then leaned forward to stroke Miss Molly's neck. 'Easy, girl!' she breathed.

'Bomb-proof, huh?' Martin Hearne muttered, standing in the gateway, arms crossed, shaking his head.

'Everyone knows you shouldn't spook a pony that way!' It was early evening and Keira still hadn't calmed down. She was talking to Red Star, taking out her anger on the forkfuls of clean straw she was banking up around the walls of his stall. She whisked the straw into the air then flattened it with firm thumps with the back of the pitchfork. 'What did he expect – that Miss Molly would just ignore the gate flying open in front of her face?'

'Still angry, huh?' Allyson spoke from across the aisle. She was bedding down her own horse, Captain, for the night and when she'd finished filling the water bucket she came to join Keira. 'You need to lighten up a little,' she advised. 'Sure, Martin Hearne was thoughtless, but I'd bet he didn't spook Miss Molly on purpose.'

'He sounded pretty mad with her,' Keira insisted. 'All that stuff about her spooking too easy and maybe she wasn't a pony they could trust.' She recalled how Mr Hearne had gone back to being grumpy the way he'd been on his first visit.

'How about we give Red Star some space?' her mom suggested, taking the fork from Keira and leading her out of the stall. 'Sometimes the owners need as much training as the ponies,' she went on with a wry grin. 'Surely you know that by now.'

Luckily the blip that happened during the Hearnes'
visit didn't spoil Jacob's training schedule for Miss
Molly.

On the Sunday, Brooke rode her out along the
Jeep trail with Keira and Red Star. It was a clear,
sunny day with frost on the ground and a thin layer
of ice covering the creek from bank to bank.

Red Star happily took the lead, stepping out
with a spring in his stride while Miss Molly tucked
in close behind. Every step brought a new challenge
– the branches that swayed and rustled in the breeze
made her wary, each root could be a snake lying
in wait, squirrels scampering across the trail

could spell danger.

'Don't be scared,' Brooke said softly. 'Squirrels are tiny – they're not gonna hurt you!'

Still Miss Molly edged forward with her ears pricked and her nostrils flared, suspicious of every twig and every blade of grass.

'Good boy, Red Star – good job!' Keira praised her pony for easing Miss Molly through her first ride in open country. When they reached the Chilli Bowl – a wide, circular hollow beneath Navajo Rock – she reined him back. 'No racing!' she warned as her lively pony itched to gallop through the sandy dip and up the far bank. 'Today we take it easy and show Miss Molly the safe way home.'

Now the days were flying by – Monday saw Jacob back in the round pen with Miss Molly and only Popcorn as a spectator, while Brooke and Keira took lessons with their mom inside the house. Tuesday morning the same, and then a trail ride for the girls up to Dolphin Rock in the afternoon. 'Who wants to ride Miss Molly?' Jacob asked them over lunch.

'Me!' Keira and Brooke answered together.

'It's Keira's turn,' Allyson decided.

So they went and brought Miss Molly and Annie in from the meadow.

'Sorry, Red Star,' Keira murmured as he followed them to the gate. 'Not this time, OK.'

He gave a long stare then tossed his mane, turned and galloped away. *See if I care!*

He was still ignoring Keira when she and Brooke set off with Miss Molly and Annie along the trail, and again when they rode the ponies back home.

'Sorry,' Keira told him again when she bedded him down in his stall for the night. 'But this is what we do here at Black Pearl Ranch – we train new ponies. It's our job!'

CHAPTER FIVE

'Miss Molly is still doing great,' Allyson told Caroline Hearne on the phone on Wednesday evening. 'We're totally happy with her progress.'

It was all going according to plan – they were almost at the end of the two week training programme.

The next day was Thursday and Keira was hoping that she wouldn't run into Sable in school, certain that she'd have more problems keeping the BIG secret. Luckily Sable was off school that day and the next.

'She had a bad asthma attack,' Lisa told Keira on Friday. 'I called her last night and she said she was sick. I only hope she's better for her birthday on Sunday.'

'Maybe she won't be well enough to come to the ranch tomorrow,' Keira confided in Brooke as they rode the bus home. 'That's when the Hearnes plan to collect Miss Molly.'

'But we'll be ready anyway,' Brooke insisted. 'We'll be out there early, brushing Sable Hearne's pony and combing her until she shines!'

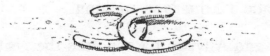

'So today is your big day!' Keira told Miss Molly.

She and Brooke had done as they'd planned – got up early and brought the little sorrel mare from the meadow into the corral straight after breakfast. They'd spent a whole hour grooming her and getting her ready. Now her chestnut coat gleamed, her hooves were polished and her mane and tail shone like silk.

'Today you travel to your new home. The Hearnes will arrive with their trailer any time now,' Keira explained.

'Hey, here they come!' Brooke heard the rattle of a vehicle approaching down the rough track and then she saw it appear round the bend. 'I hope Sable made it – this is so exciting!'

Jacob and Allyson had spotted the visitors too

and they came out of the house. By the time the trailer pulled up in the yard, the whole Lucas family was waiting there to greet them.

'I love this moment and I hate it,' Keira confessed to Brooke as she put the brushes and combs to one side. Love – hate, love – hate; she see-sawed between the two.

Brooke agreed. The girls were proud of the work they and their dad had put in on Miss Molly yet sad that today was the day she would leave. So they held their breaths, hoping that the Hearnes would be happy with what they saw.

Caroline Hearne was the first to step down from the trailer, followed soon after by her husband, all smiles today because of the surprise he'd planned for his daughter. Then Sable appeared.

She slid down from the cab dressed in jeans and brand new cowboy boots – a pale shade of purple with fancy contrasting leather piping – boots that must have cost a fortune, Keira thought. Sable looked pale and confused as she took in the house, the yard and the corral where Miss Molly stood.

'Go with Keira and Brooke, honey!' her mom

urged as the adults shook hands with Jacob and Allyson. 'The girls have something very special to show you.'

Keira felt her stomach tighten. This was it – the big moment. She led the way into the corral and rested a hand on Miss Molly's sleek neck.

'This is your big birthday surprise!' Sable's dad called.

Sable hesitated as she drew close to Miss Molly. Brooke joined Keira and waited nervously for Sable's reaction.

Miss Molly turned her pretty head and looked straight at Sable, fixing her new owner with those gorgeous brown eyes.

'Happy birthday, honey!' Mr and Mrs Hearne called from the yard.

Sable gazed at Miss Molly and her eyes filled with tears.

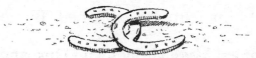

'Happy tears,' Caroline Hearne explained to Allyson at the gate to the corral. Meanwhile, Martin Hearne and Jacob prepared to lead Miss Molly into the trailer. 'Honestly, she had no idea we'd bought her a pony. And she's longed for this for ages!'

'What do you think? Don't you just love her?' Keira asked Sable. 'She's by far the prettiest pony we've ever had here at Black Pearl Ranch!'

'Is she really mine?' Sable hung back, wiping her tears and shaking her head in disbelief.

'She really is!' Brooke's smile went from ear to ear.

'Dad always said ponies were too much work.'

'He changed his mind. I reckon your mom persuaded him,' Brooke explained. By now Jacob had unhitched Miss Molly's lead rope and handed it to Martin Hearne, who began to lead her through the gate towards the trailer.

'Take it slow and easy,' Jacob advised.

Sable's dad didn't seem to hear. He strode on, and when the pony started to resist and pull back he straightaway jerked hard on the rope.

Don't do that! Keira drew a sharp breath. *You'll scare her and she won't co-operate!*

'Quit it!' Mr Hearne snapped at Miss Molly, tugging again.

Miss Molly's ears went back; she dug in her heels.

'What's happening?' Mrs Hearne asked anxiously.

'Martin, why not let Jacob handle this?' Allyson called. Then she turned back to Caroline. 'It looks like there may be a problem getting Miss Molly into the trailer.'

Or else she hates Mr Hearne, Keira thought. *And who can blame her?*

It was then, in the split second when this passed through Keira's mind, that the situation exploded out of control. She didn't see every detail – it happened much too fast – but Mr Hearne seemed to grab the loose end of the long lead rope and whip it down across the pony's back. Pain shot through Miss Molly and she reared up high, snatching the rope clean out of the man's hands.

'Martin!' Keira heard Mrs Hearne's frightened yell and she saw her run towards her husband. She felt Sable freeze to the spot. Her mom and Brooke set off after Mrs Hearne.

Caroline was at Martin's side, Miss Molly was still rearing on her hind legs, her front hooves flailing high in the air.

'Step back!' Jacob warned, striding between the Hearnes and the pony, his arms stretched wide.

Thud! Keira heard Miss Molly's hooves land, saw

her dad stagger sideways and fall to the ground. Her heart missed a beat.

Then her mom reached the spot as Miss Molly whirled away and set off at a crazy canter around the yard. The Hearnes stood helpless as Jacob fell unconscious, with Allyson crouched over him.

'Girls, open the gate, let the pony back into the corral!' Allyson yelled. 'And Martin and Caroline, please stand back, give me some room. Everyone, do as I say!'

CHAPTER SIX

Brooke opened the gate and Miss Molly galloped through.

Allyson bent over Jacob. She leaned forward to listen to his breathing. 'Call 911,' she told Caroline Hearne. 'We need an ambulance.'

Keira drew a long, ragged breath. Her heart pounded, her head swam and she only just made it across the yard to be with her mom.

'Stupid pony!' Martin Hearne muttered as he

recovered from the shock. 'Now look what she's done.'

'Will Dad be OK?' Keira whispered.

Gently, Allyson removed Jacob's broad-brimmed Stetson and placed it beside him on the ground. 'His breathing's fine, but he took a blow to the side of his head. It knocked him out cold.'

Keira stared in horror at the bleeding cut made by the edge of Miss Molly's hoof – three or four centimetres long and just above her dad's left ear. His eyes were closed, his face drained of colour.

Back in the corral, Miss Molly had galloped herself into a terrified sweat.

'Sable, you come out of there!' Martin Hearne yelled. 'I want you to climb into the trailer, out of harm's way!'

Slowly Sable followed her dad's orders. She passed close to where Jacob lay and, as Keira glanced up, she mouthed a single word – 'Sorry!'

Keira nodded and tried to swallow – her throat hurt, she was trying so hard to hold back the tears.

'OK, he's waking up!' Allyson sighed as Jacob began to stir.

Keira's dad moved his head and groaned. Then his eyelids began to flicker open.

'Keira, your dad's going to be OK. You need to help your sister calm down Miss Molly and tie her to a rail.'

'And we need to get Sable out of here,' Martin Hearne decided. 'Caroline, you made the call to the emergency services?'

Mrs Hearne nodded. 'They're sending an

ambulance from Sheriton. It'll take maybe an hour to get here.'

By now Jacob's eyes were wide open and he was trying to raise himself from the ground. But the pain was too much. He drew a sharp breath then sank back down.

'Don't try to move,' Allyson ordered. She

glanced up at the Hearnes. 'It's OK – you go,' she said quietly.

'We should stay,' Caroline argued, 'at least until the paramedics get here.'

'No, take care of your daughter.' Allyson was calm and firm. 'I'll call you later.'

'What are we supposed to tell Sable about her birthday present?' Martin wanted to know. 'Do we say her pony is no good – she freaks out at any little thing?'

Caroline tried to step in. 'Not now, Martin.'

Jacob lay on the ground, looking up at the couple. 'There has to be a reason for the way Miss Molly reacted,' he said through his pain.

'Yeah, she's nuts,' Martin Hearne grunted. He rolled his eyes towards the heavens. 'We made a bad choice the day we bought her – end of story!'

The Hearnes left Black Pearl Ranch without Miss
Molly. Their trailer rattled up the dirt track, leaving
Brooke and Keira to tie the sorrel pony to a rail
while Allyson talked Jacob through events.

'The way you're having trouble moving, it looks like you cracked a rib,' she told him. 'The ambulance will be here soon and they'll take you to the hospital.'

'No hospital,' Jacob protested, struggling to get up.

'Lie still. Yes – hospital. You'll need an X-ray to see if the rib is broken, plus they'll check you out for concussion and put some sutures in that cut.'

Over in the corral, Keira and Brooke did their best to calm Miss Molly. 'Easy!' Keira whispered as she tethered her to a rail. 'No one's gonna hurt you. Mr Hearne's gone away.'

Brooke shook her head. 'This wasn't totally his fault,' she pointed out.

'It *so* was! Keira had seen it with her own eyes –

the way Sable's dad had heaved on the rope then raised the end over his head to lash it down across the pony's back.

'I think it was something else.' Brooke ran her hand down Miss Molly's neck. The pony's coat was dark and rough with sweat and she was trembling all over.

'Like what?' Keira wondered. But this wasn't the time to figure it out – they had to get the pony into her stall, give her water and leave her to get over her trauma. Meanwhile, they had their dad to worry about too.

'I can't take time off work,' Jacob was insisting after the girls had taken care of Miss Molly. He'd raised himself from the ground and was standing doubled over, in spite of what Allyson had said.

The girls' mom took out a handkerchief to dab at the blood on his face. 'Jacob, you don't have a choice. You have to rest up and let me and the kids run the place for a while.'

'Dad, I hear the ambulance!' Brooke picked up a distant sound of an engine. 'Mom's right – you have to stop in the hospital and do what the doctors tell you.'

As he tried to straighten up, Jacob groaned. 'I hear you. And listen, girls, I need you to take good care of Miss Molly while I'm away.'

'We will,' Keira promised. The ambulance appeared at the top of the hill and sped towards them. 'Dad, what happened back there – it wasn't her fault, was it?'

'It never is,' he agreed. 'There's always a reason

why a pony acts up, if only we're tuned in enough to see it.'

'So we need to find out.' There wasn't much time – the paramedics had arrived and Allyson was leading Jacob slowly towards the ambulance with Keira and Brooke on either side. 'Don't worry, Dad, we'll do it,' she promised. 'We'll work this out, you can bet your life on it.'

'They want to keep your dad in hospital for a couple of days,' Allyson reported. It was late Saturday evening, and a raw, cold wind was blowing off the dark mountains. 'The X-ray showed he did crack a rib, but the lung isn't punctured. Now they need to do a head scan to check the damage there.'

Keira gazed at her mom's tired face and said nothing.

'Mrs Hearne called,' Brooke told Allyson. 'She said for you to call her back.'

Keira and Brooke sat in silence in the kitchen as Allyson went off to make the call.

'So there goes Sable's surprise present,' Keira said at last. She sat with Popcorn on her lap, absent-mindedly stroking him. 'Now they'll never take Miss Molly home.'

Brooke sighed. For a while it seemed hopeless until she spoke again. 'Unless we work out exactly what went wrong, like you told Dad we would.'

Keira agreed. 'He says there's always a reason and I believe him. But what ideas do you have?'

'I'm not sure. Let's think back to when it happened. What did you see?'

'I saw Mr Hearne try to drag Miss Molly towards the trailer. I saw him raise the end of the rope to whip her.'

'You did?' Brooke exclaimed. 'I saw it differently. I reckon he totally panicked – I don't think he planned to whip her. And you remember how close they were to the trailer when it happened? Doesn't that remind you of how Miss Molly acted when she first arrived?'

Keira thought back. 'Yeah, she was kind of spooked coming down the ramp.'

'Exactly, both times it was the trailer!' Brooke felt she was on to something.

Keira took up the train of thought. 'You know – if Miss Molly does have a problem loading on and off trailers, maybe Reed was right. Maybe Miss Molly is the same pony that belonged to the Allens.'

Brooke stood up and began to pace the floor. 'You mean, even way back then Miss Molly had developed a trailer problem? Maybe she thinks that a trailer is some kind of trap – it's too dark and narrow, it spells danger. And it only takes one bad experience to spook a pony for life.'

'We should visit Reed, talk to him about it,' Keira decided. She pushed Popcorn from her lap then joined Brooke at the window where they both gazed up at the night sky. They thought of their dad in hospital, of poor Sable back home minus her birthday surprise. And they thought of Miss Molly shut up in her stall, unwanted by her new owners, her whole future uncertain.

'Tomorrow,' Brooke said firmly. 'We get up early and we ride out to visit Reed.'

CHAPTER SEVEN

A low, cold mist hung over the valley when Keira and Brooke saddled Red Star and Annie next morning. The ponies stood patiently in the corral, their warm breaths clouding the air.

'Did Mom call the hospital?' Brooke asked as she tightened Annie's cinch.

'Yep. They told her they only want to keep Dad one more night. She can bring him home tomorrow.' Though the weather was dreary, Keira felt more cheerful after a good night's sleep. She was sure that between them, she, Reed and Brooke would be able to get to the bottom of Miss Molly's hang-up over trailers.

'But remember that Dad won't be back at work right away,' Brooke pointed out. 'And I looked at his diary – he has two new ponies coming in on Tuesday.'

Keira slipped Red Star's bit between his teeth. She refused to look on the dark side, even though she knew that money at Black Pearl Ranch was always tight. 'So we can do the hands-on work with the ponies while Dad gives instructions.'

'Gotcha.' Brooke grinned then swung into the saddle. 'That's a 24-7 commitment you just made, leave aside the school work we have to do, plus the usual ranch chores, the housework, the …'

'Yeah, yeah!' Keira mounted Red Star and headed out of the corral. 'So let's go see Reed,' she insisted. 'The sooner we sort out the Miss Molly problem the better.'

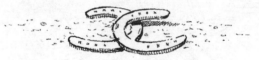

Keira and Brooke trotted their ponies out by the meadow, along the Jeep trail. As they rode the mist lifted from the mountains, giving them a clear view of steep, frost-covered hillsides.

Keira soon settled into the bouncing rhythm of Red Star's brisk trot, enjoying the crisp sound of his hooves striking the frozen ground. Glancing sideways at Brooke, who kept pace on Annie,

she smiled. 'Hey, did I ever tell you that I'm glad you're my big sister?'

'Whoa!' Brooke raised her eyebrows then grinned back. 'Can I put that on record and use it against you next time we get into a fight?'

Keira laughed. Her spirits were high as they trotted the trail. She planned ahead for the rest of the day – number one: meet with Reed and find out more about the Allens' experience with Miss Molly, number two: talk to Jay Allen on the phone, number three: find out exactly what went wrong so that she and Brooke could set Miss Molly on a retraining programme.

It was left to Brooke to sound a cautious note. 'Don't get your hopes up too high,' she warned. 'Even if we re-school Miss Molly to stay calm around trailers, that doesn't mean for certain that the Hearnes will still take her.'

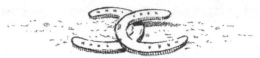

'So you admit it – I was right!' Reed enjoyed making Keira blush. 'This was the same pony all along!'

'So I was wrong.' Keira scuffed the pointed toe of her boot in the dirt of the Walters' corral. She moved on quickly. 'Reed, how well do you know Jay Allen?'

'Well enough to make a phone call, I guess.' Grinning at Brooke, Reed invited the girls into the ranch house where they found his dad, Tom, frying bacon and eggs for breakfast.

'Want to join us?' Tom asked.

Keira never said no to rashers of crispy bacon between two slices of fresh bread. Soon everyone was seated around the kitchen table and as they ate, Reed picked up the phone.

'Hey, Jay,' he began after he'd dialled the number. 'It's Reed here. I wanted to ask you about a sorrel mare you once owned ...'

'So?' Keira and Brooke faced Reed across the table. They'd picked up a few facts from the one-sided phone conversation, but the picture was still unclear.

'Miss Molly went by a different name when she was at Jay's place,' Reed told them. 'Back then, I reckon almost three years ago, her papers named her as Brown Velvet.'

'Miss Molly suits her better,' Keira said firmly.

'So Jay owned her all that time?' Brooke checked.

'Almost. He says they tried real hard with her. Jay and his older brother don't give up easily.'

Keira took hold of the edge of the table to steady her nerves and to keep the tension out of her voice. 'And the exact problem was …?'

'She was hard to load on and off a trailer,' Reed confirmed. 'In fact, Jay says she was worse than hard – she was darned near impossible.'

'Which means Jay could never take her along to compete in the local rodeos and reining competitions,' Brooke guessed. 'That would be a big negative as far as he was concerned.'

'Right. But Brown Velvet came with good breeding papers and his brother paid a high price, so I reckon they wanted to keep her in spite of the trailer problem ...'

'But?' Keira interrupted.

'Yeah, there's a big "but" coming. Something real bad happened in spring this year. Jay's big brother, Luke, had the idea that he would have one last try to get the pony into a trailer, but even with the help of a blindfold and some ropes around her, they still didn't make it.'

'Why? What went wrong?' Brooke wanted to know.

'Brown Velvet reared up and came down right on Luke's foot – broke two bones.'

Keira took a deep breath. 'And that was it – the

Allens sold her to the Hearnes?'

'Nope.' Reed stood up to help his dad clear the plates. 'Luke tried all summer long but he couldn't find a private buyer. Come September, he sold her to a dealer in Manning Junction, just this side of the Interstate.'

CHAPTER EIGHT

'JLK Horse Dealer.' Keira read the sign above the entrance to the yard. She spotted a small, white-painted house at the end of a hundred-metre drive, and beside the house a large barn with open doors.

'The place looks OK,' Tom Walters said as he drove his Ford truck down the track. 'The guy who runs this keeps a neat yard and barn.'

As soon as he'd finished his chores at the Three

Horseshoes, Tom had listened to Reed's request to drive him, Brooke and Keira out to Manning Junction to visit a horse dealer they'd found in the phone book. 'Tell me what you're hoping to find,' he'd said.

'It's the only horse dealership in town and the girls want to check it out,' Reed explained. 'Their dad is in hospital with a broken rib because of a pony that was sold out of there.'

It was the first Tom had heard of Jacob's accident and he quickly agreed to help. But now he was surprised by the well-kept outfit. 'It doesn't look like the kind of place that would sell a third-rate pony.'

'Let's wait and see.' When Reed saw a figure emerge from the barn, he jumped down from the truck, soon followed by Keira, Brooke and his dad.

The man strode towards them, ready to shake Tom's hand. He was tall, with a full head of short white hair and a white moustache, a lined face and hands that looked like he'd known hard work all his life. 'J. L. King.' He introduced himself to his visitors in a deep, slow voice. 'Are you guys here to buy a pony?'

'Maybe.' Tom took his time. 'We'd sure like to see what you have to sell, if that's OK.'

'That's my job,' Mr King replied in his easy, relaxed way. 'I keep all my stock inside the barn now that winter's here. Just follow me.'

As Keira followed the owner into the barn she noticed that there were two younger guys at work. One wore jeans and an old denim jacket with the frayed collar turned up. The other, who kept his back turned as he shovelled grain pellets into a wheelbarrow, was dressed in a black sweatshirt. Neither man stopped what he was doing as the group walked by.

'What colour pony are you looking for?' Mr King wanted to know. 'I have a pretty paint gelding down the far end of the barn, just two years old, never had a saddle on him. Or if you want something with some miles on it already, I have an Appaloosa mare – four years old, all the paperwork correct and in good order.'

'Let's take a look at the paint,' Tom suggested, walking ahead with Mr King and leaving the others to poke around the barn.

'Dad's right – this place looks OK,' Reed muttered to Keira as Brooke split off to check an area lined with stalls and wooden mangers.

Keira noticed the guy in the sweatshirt stop work then stare at them through narrowed eyes. She screwed up her courage and walked over to him. 'Hey, we're looking for a pony,' she began.

The man nodded but said nothing, resting on the shovel he'd been using.

'There's one pony we heard about but we don't see her anywhere,' Keira went on.

Quickly Reed realised what she was up to. 'Yeah, a little sorrel with a white flash down her nose,' he added. 'A friend of mine brought her along here a couple of months back.'

'Gone,' the man said, ready to turn away again.

'But you know the pony we're talking about?' Keira insisted. 'We heard she was real pretty.'

'Hey, Spencer, that must be Brown Velvet – the mare from the Allens' place.' The man in the denim jacket had overheard and seemed more ready to talk to the visitors. 'Sorry folks, you're a couple of weeks too late. The boss did all he could to find a new home for her, but there was a history …'

'What kind of a history?' Keira jumped in.

'Some problems loading her into a trailer. She had to be sedated every time you took her within spitting distance. The plain fact is, people won't buy a pony with trailer issues. So Mr King got rid of her, ain't that right, Spencer?'

'That's right,' the other man grunted.

'Got rid of her?' It was Reed's turn to ask the question. 'You mean, she went for horse meat?'

'No way.' The helpful worker shook his head. 'Mr King doesn't trade with the slaughterhouse guys. As far as I know, he gave that problem pony away to a woman who runs a sanctuary two hours north from here. That's what we do with stock we can't sell.'

Keira breathed a sigh of relief. *Thank heavens!* But then again, the story didn't fit – they knew for a fact that Miss Molly wasn't at the sanctuary. So how come?

'OK, kids, time to leave.' Just then Tom Walters came back. He gathered Brooke, Keira and Reed by the barn door and thanked Mr King for showing them his stock. 'I liked the paint but he doesn't quite fit the bill,' he said as they shook hands once more.

'Well, come back and see us any time you're in the area,' the owner told him. 'And if I happen to be busy out at my other dealership in Sinclair County, just ask my second-in-command, Spencer here, to show you around.'

'He couldn't have been more helpful,' was Tom

Walters' opinion of J. L. King. He shared it with
Allyson over a cup of coffee at Black Pearl Ranch.
'Mr King runs a good, honest business, if you ask me.'

Allyson thought for a while then turned to Keira.
'Not what you expected to find, huh?'

'No, but there's still something weird,' Keira
insisted. 'I mean, who decided to change Brown
Velvet's name to Miss Molly, and how come she isn't

at the pony sanctuary like the guy at the dealership claimed?'

'I have no idea.' Her mom took a sip of coffee. 'But you know what, honey – maybe it doesn't matter. After all, we have to focus on curing Miss Molly's problem, not turning detective and trying to solve mysteries.'

Tom Walters agreed. 'It'll take a heap of patience and hard work to get the pony right, but there has to be a way.'

'We sure can't sedate Miss Molly every time, and no way do we blindfold ponies and rope them into a trailer,' Brooke said. 'That's not what we do.'

'No force – no whips, no ropes.' Keira thought for a while. 'There's always food – maybe we could coax her in with treats.'

'Let's try that tomorrow morning while Mom brings Dad home from the hospital,' Brooke suggested.

It felt good to be planning ahead but Keira was still worried. Leaving the others to talk, she went outside and across the dark yard into the barn. She turned on the light and walked down the quiet aisle, reaching over stall doors to pat first Misty and then Captain. 'How are you all doing?' she murmured.

Hearing her voice, Red Star came to his door.

'Hey you,' she whispered. 'Sorry we didn't get to ride today, only I've been busy. You know we have this big problem with Miss Molly?'

Red Star lowered his head to nuzzle her palm.

'Well, we figured maybe someone had been cruel to her at the horse dealership out at Manning

Junction, but when we took a look at the place there didn't seem to be a thing wrong with it.'

Red Star cocked his head to one side as if he was thinking hard.

'Right. So what do we do next? We could go and talk to Jay Allen, but Mom says we shouldn't waste time. We should forget what happened in the past and look ahead.'

Her pony tossed his mane from his face. *Maybe she's right.*

'But I still say we should work out what went wrong before the Hearnes bought Miss Molly. Only, maybe there isn't enough time. Mom's too busy, what with Dad being out of action.'

Red Star looked Keira in the eye and then glanced sideways towards Miss Molly's stall. *Go and talk to her, why don't you?*

Good idea. Patting his neck, she walked on down the aisle. 'Hey, Miss Molly, I wish you could speak out and tell me exactly what spooks you.'

The little sorrel looked unhappy as she appeared at her door. She swished her tail nervously as Keira approached.

'Don't worry – I know it's not your fault that Dad got hurt,' Keira said quietly. 'And now we realise you hate all trailers. We *will* work on it, I promise.'

Miss Molly took a deep breath that filled her lungs and came out as a sigh.

'Yeah,' Keira agreed. The dim yellow light in the barn cast long shadows and the only noise came from Red Star sinking sleepily into his straw bed. 'It's tough, and I know how you feel,' she murmured to Miss

Molly. 'Today is Sable Hearne's birthday and you were her big surprise. I'm sorry it didn't work out.'

The sad little sorrel turned her head away.

Keira reached out to stroke her. 'Don't worry, if it turns out the Hearnes really don't want you, I'll find you the best home I can,' she whispered. 'Cross my heart I will!'

CHAPTER NINE

'It's no good – her head is really messed up.'

Brooke stepped down from the Black Pearl trailer parked in the yard close to the corral fence. She and Keira had been working with Miss Molly for two whole hours – ever since their mom had left for Sheriton. 'Her problem goes way back, remember.'

'We never said it would be easy,' Keira reminded her. She stood twenty metres from the trailer, holding Miss Molly on a short lead rope to stop her prancing and backing away. For the last thirty minutes Brooke had been waiting inside the trailer with a bucket filled with a mix of grain pellets and

chopped carrot, but even this treat hadn't brought the sorrel within ten paces of the ramp.

Now Brooke set the bucket down on the ground

and leaned wearily against the fence. 'I hear the phone!' she said, cocking an ear before sprinting towards the house.

'He-ey!' Keira sighed. She stroked Miss Molly's neck as she gazed through the fence rails at Red Star stamping his feet and blowing clouds of warm breath into the frosty air. He was loosely tethered to a post beside the red barn door, sniffing at the ground and hoping to pick up stray wisps of alfalfa which had fallen from a nearby bale. 'OK, Red Star, so what do we do next?' she asked him.

He raised his head to look across at her and suddenly, as if by magic, she knew she had the answer!

'That was a call from Sable,' Brooke reported when she came back out of the house. 'She waited until her dad left home then she dialled our number to ask for an update on Miss Molly.'

'What did you tell her?' Keira asked.

'That her pony was fine and we were still working with her.'

'Cool.'

'Not so cool,' Brooke sighed. 'Sable said she had another asthma attack soon after they left here on Saturday. Now her dad's convinced that on top of Miss Molly's trailer problem, Sable is allergic to horses.'

'That sucks,' Keira sighed. But she was still impatient to share her latest idea. 'Listen, Brooke, I think I know what we need to do!'

'You do?' It was clear that Brooke felt they'd tried everything and nothing had worked.

Eagerly Keira told Brooke to open the gate into the corral. 'Go fetch Red Star for me. I'll wait here with Miss Molly.'

A minute later, Brooke returned with Red Star.

'OK, load him in the trailer,' Keira instructed. 'Go ahead, Red Star – show Miss Molly there's nothing to be scared of.'

Brooke nodded brightly and went ahead with Red Star up the ramp. He stepped jauntily, flicking his ears towards the nervous sorrel, letting her know there was no reason to hold back.

Miss Molly watched him carefully. She heard his hooves ring out on the metal ramp and saw him disappear inside the dark box.

'See, no monster is hiding in there to get you!' Keira murmured. 'And if Red Star can do it, so can you!'

Very slowly she began to lead Miss Molly towards the trailer. This time they got within three or four steps of the ramp but then the sorrel changed her mind. She raised her head, whinnied and pulled back.

Straight away Keira took off the pressure. She stood quietly beside Miss Molly while Red Star came to the trailer door and poked out his head. When he saw that she was still afraid, he walked down the ramp, straight over to where she stood.

'Tell her, Red Star,' Keira whispered.

For a few seconds Red Star stood nose to nose with Miss Molly then he gave a quick toss of his head, turned and walked back towards the ramp. One step, two steps – he halted and waited.

Miss Molly hesitated for what seemed like forever then took a small step after him.

'Good girl!' Keira breathed. 'Again!'

One more small, scared step and Miss Molly stood right behind Red Star.

'Go ahead now,' Keira gently urged her pony,

standing close beside Miss Molly.

Step number three and Red Star's front hooves were on the ramp. *Come on, Miss Molly, follow me!*

Miss Molly braced herself. She edged forward.

Four, five, six steps and Red Star was in the trailer.

Miss Molly quivered from head to foot. She peered into the dark, musty space, took courage from Red Star and walked in after him. Four, five, six steps to victory!

Keira punched the air with a jubilant fist. They were in the trailer with Brooke and Red Star. She was stroking Miss Molly's neck.

'Totally cool!' Brooke sighed.

'Good job, Keira.' Jacob arrived home from the hospital to see Miss Molly calmly loading on and off the trailer.

'I have no idea how you did that.' Allyson gave a disbelieving smile.

'I didn't – Red Star did!' Delighted, Keira told her mom and dad exactly what had happened.

'But it was your idea,' Brooke pointed out. 'We'd spent all morning trying different ways of loading Miss Molly before you had your breakthrough.'

Jacob listened thoughtfully. His face was still pale, though the cut was already healing. 'I'm proud of you, Keira. You can do my job any day you like.'

Wow! Keira's heart seemed to swell until she thought it would burst.

'I mean it – you have a talent. You have the rare

trick of thinking the way a horse thinks – you put yourself in his place.'

Wow again! Now the proud tears welled up and she couldn't stop them.

'Put these two ponies out in the meadow,' Allyson told the girls quietly. 'Then come in the house and sit with your dad. He has to take things easy for a couple of weeks, remember.'

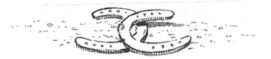

That evening a log fire blazed in the hearth and the lamp on the low coffee table gave off a warm glow. Jacob sat with his feet up, happy for once to let the others fetch him hot chocolate and cookies.

'Tomorrow we get the two new ponies,' Allyson reminded him. 'They arrive soon after breakfast, so the kids and I need to be up early.'

'But you can stay in bed,' Brooke added. 'We mean it, Dad – you have to follow doctors' orders.'

'Maybe, maybe not,' he grumbled.

'Da-ad!' Keira warned. 'You said I could take over your job any time I liked!'

'Not quite this soon.' Jacob smiled then leaned sideways for his chocolate and groaned. 'Ouch!'

'See!' Brooke and Keira chorused.

Just then the phone rang and Keira answered it. It took her a while to recognise Lisa Shaw's voice.

'Keira, is that you? Listen, I just came off the phone to Sable. She's totally heartbroken. I had to talk to somebody about it.'

'Lisa? What's up?'

'Sable – she's devastated. She says her dad once

and for all said no to her having that birthday pony.'

Keira's heart lurched. 'But things have changed. We solved Miss Molly's trailer problem. Wait until Mr Hearne hears – he'll soon change his mind.'

Frowning, Brooke came over to listen in to the conversation.

'Sable's dad won't shift,' Lisa insisted. 'You could tell him that pony is the sure-fire winner of the next Kentucky Derby and he'll still say the same thing – they don't want Miss Molly, end of story.'

Brooke seized the phone from a shocked Keira. 'There's something else besides the trailer problem, isn't there?' she demanded. 'Lisa, what do you know that we don't?'

There was a long pause then the voice on the

other end of the phone delivered the final blow. 'Mr Hearne brought in the family doctor and he confirmed one hundred per cent that Sable *is* allergic to horses.'

'Seriously?' Brooke whispered.

'I'm totally serious. Every time Sable goes near a pony she'll have an asthma attack. The doctor says it's so bad that one day it might even kill her.'

CHAPTER TEN

'Who knows? Maybe it's for the best?'

Early next morning Brooke led Annie out to the meadow with Keira and Red Star. Neither girl had slept much for worrying about the latest news on poor Sable.

'How can it be good?' Keira argued. 'It's the end of Sable's pony dream, plus it leaves Miss Molly with no home to go to.'

Once through the meadow gate, the girls stopped

and took off the ponies' lead ropes. Annie set off across the frosty grass at an easy lope. Red Star tossed his head and exploded into a flat-out gallop.

'Yes, but none of the Hearnes knows anything about ponies,' Brooke pointed out. 'I mean – they know zilch. Even if Sable didn't have asthma, what kind of owners would they have made?'

Keira recalled Sable's expensive, brand new cowboy boots and sighed. 'But I do feel sorry for her.'

'Me too.'

'And what happens to Miss Molly now? That's what really scares me.'

'She could go to the pony sanctuary, I guess.' Brooke's suggestion came with a shrug and a sigh.

Keira walked in silence for a while. She pictured gorgeous, lively Miss Molly penned into a corral with a bunch of old and broken-down ponies – it would be a peaceful life, but boring. 'She deserves better,' she muttered as she turned back towards the corral. 'And I'm gonna make sure she gets it.'

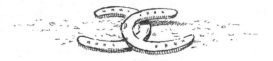

There was no time for Keira to plan her next move, however, because a trailer was arriving with the two new ponies and Allyson was there in the yard issuing orders to the driver.

'Back up!' she yelled, waving her arms until the trailer was parked close to the fence. 'OK, good! Switch off the engine. And Brooke, open up the barn door. Keira, stand by with extra lead ropes, in case we need them.'

Soon the trailer ramp was lowered and the driver led out the first pony – an easy-going grey gelding who came down the ramp like a lamb and let himself be led straight into the barn. Then Allyson brought out the second visitor – a sturdy brown and white paint with a thick white mane and tail. The paint raised her head to sniff the air, saw the grey gelding disappear into the barn then eagerly followed.

'Nice and easy does it,' Allyson commented once the new arrivals were safely stalled. 'Give us a couple of weeks with these two guys and we'll hand you back two solid kids' rides, no problem.'

As Allyson and the driver got chatting about Jacob's recent accident, she took him over to the house, leaving Keira and Brooke to make sure that the new ponies were settled into their stalls.

'I'll bring grain, you bring water,' Brooke told Keira.

So Keira filled two buckets and carried them down the aisle, passing Miss Molly's stall on the way.

Miss Molly appeared at the door, looking longingly at Keira.

'I know,' she murmured. 'You want to be out in the meadow with Red Star and Annie, but right now I have no clue what's gonna happen to you.'

Miss Molly let out a loud sigh. With her mane falling untidily forward over her pretty face, she looked down in the dumps.

'I need to talk to dad,' Keira decided. 'It's top of my list, right after I'm through giving water to these guys!'

Allyson was working with Captain in the round pen and the house was empty when Keira went to find her dad. She looked in the living room where he was supposed to be sitting with his feet up, then upstairs, then out again on to the porch. Finally she walked round the back of the house and across the yard to the tack room where she found him cleaning and tidying bridles.

'Da-ad!' she protested. 'The doctors told you to rest.'

Jacob winked at her. 'Don't tell your mom!'

'How are you feeling?'

'Stiff and sore, but I was going stir-crazy. You know I hate being cooped up in the house.'

Keira took a deep breath. 'OK, Dad – I need to talk to you about Miss Molly.'

He went on straightening the bridles on their hooks but he let Keira know he was ready to listen.

'We had a phone call from Lisa Shaw. The Hearnes won't take their pony away from here. That's a definite.'

'I hear you.'

'And I know she spooked and that's how come you ended up in the hospital, and I wouldn't blame you if you turned your back on her ...'

'No, I won't do that,' he said steadily.

Keira bit her bottom lip then went on. 'Did Mom tell you that Reed's dad drove us out to Manning Junction to see the horse dealer there?'

Jacob nodded. At last he stopped work and gave her his full attention. 'What's on your mind, Keira?'

'There was something not right. We found out that Jay Allen and his brother sold Miss Molly to Mr King – the dealer – but she wasn't Miss Molly back then; she was Brown Velvet. And we know that Mr King couldn't find anyone who would buy her because of her trailer problem.'

'Which *you* solved,' he said with an encouraging smile.

'So, she was supposed to go off to a pony

sanctuary a couple of hours north. But it ended up that the Hearnes bought her instead.'

'With a new name and papers that said she was three years old when she was nearer five,' Jacob added. 'Yeah, that's definitely not right. So?'

'So I don't want Miss Molly to end up at the sanctuary,' Keira explained. 'And I want to find out what really happened after the Allens sold her to Mr King and before she ended up with the Hearnes.'

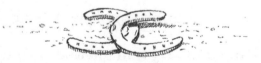

Allyson had warned Jacob that he shouldn't drive but she'd known he wouldn't listen.

'Only to Manning Junction,' he'd promised, leaning out of his truck to talk while Keira sat in the passenger seat beside him. 'Tonight I'll rest up.'

'Jacob Lucas, you're the most stubborn man on God's earth!'

'That's why you married me!' he'd joked, wincing a little as he'd eased the lever into Drive and left the yard.

'Let me do the talking,' he told Keira as they approached the dealership.

'And I'll sneak off and take a look around,' she agreed.

They could see the JLK Horse Dealer sign a hundred metres ahead and the white house set back from the road. Jacob signalled left and turned down the straight track.

Keira remembered it all – the neat house and porch, the tidy yard, the big barn. And she recognised the figure in the old denim jacket who stood at the barn door watching them pull up.

'Karl Hamlin,' he told Jacob, coming forward and offering his hand as Keira's dad stepped gingerly from his truck. 'Mr King's not here, but I can show you around.'

'I appreciate it,' Jacob said. 'This is my girl, Keira – she dropped by here a couple of days back. She told me you have an Appaloosa I might want to take a look at.'

Keira did her best to smile but she felt a tight knot in her stomach. Could she fake an interest in the ponies they had for sale, or would Karl Hamlin notice that her nerves were stretched to breaking point?

'Sure, follow me.' Luckily, Karl took Jacob at his

word and led the way through the barn. So far there was no sign of Mr King's other worker – the unsmiling one called Spencer.

'We've had a lot of interest in the Appie,' Karl was saying. 'We also have a new three-year-old bay – part mustang, part Quarter Horse. Not for a beginner but he's definitely worth you taking a look.'

Keira let Karl and her dad walk ahead. Their voices grew fainter and she seized her chance to branch out of the main part of the barn, down a linking passageway into another covered area with a dirt floor and a high roof. It looked like a small indoor arena or loading area, though it was too dark to see clearly what the space was used for.

There was a horse or a pony somewhere nearby

– of that Keira was sure. She felt the animal's presence and she heard hooves pawing the ground. Then she made out a shadowy shape in the far corner. There was a tension in the air – fear, maybe.

Gradually, her eyes got used to the gloom. Yes, it was a dark bay pony, tightly tethered to an iron hook on the wall, and there was a man coming up from behind, holding a heavy cloth sack in his hand. It was the man in black, the one called Spencer.

Keira stepped out of sight behind a metal bin used for storing grain. She saw that the pony's body was dark with sweat, that the man was flapping the sack in his face and the pony was tied too tight to back away.

Stop! she wanted to cry. But her own fear pinned her to the spot.

Spencer flapped the sack against the pony's neck and all against his back and haunches. Wildly the pony tried to rear and buck. He turned his head to bite his attacker but once again the rope was too taut. *Flap!* The man beat the sack against the pony. The pony kicked out with his hind feet. *Flap!* Again the sack landed on his back, *flap-flap!* – on his neck and head.

And now Keira did come out from behind the container and called out for Spencer to stop. Just as she did so, the pony stretched the rope to breaking point. It snapped and the pony bucked and kicked free. Spencer dropped the sack and jumped back. Keira yelled for her dad. Footsteps came running.

'Dad, through here!'

The pony reared
and struck out with
his hooves. Spencer
sprinted
across the
arena
towards the
exit. He
wasn't fast enough –
the pony, driven wild by the sack and the tight
tether, leaped in front of the man and reared
again. He towered over him and Spencer
staggered backwards – right into Jacob's arms.

CHAPTER ELEVEN

'D id anyone get hurt?' Karl Hamlin had come in on the tail end of the action, in time to drive the pony back across the arena. Jacob stood with his arm around Keira's shoulder while the frenzied pony galloped away.

'Everyone's fine, no thanks to your buddy here.' Jacob spoke through gritted teeth, looking angrier than Keira had ever seen him. 'It's years since I saw a guy sacking out a pony like that. The horse couldn't move on the end of this rope. No wonder he went crazy.'

Karl shook his head then pushed Spencer against the metal container. 'Is that true? What were you thinking?'

Spencer pulled himself free. 'I always sack them out when they first get here. How else do I get the kick, bite and strike out of them?'

Keira stared. She couldn't believe what Spencer was saying, though she'd read in books and magazines about the traditional way of breaking horses. For herself, she totally preferred her dad's gentler technique of join-up.

'And does your boss know about the method you use?' Jacob accused.

'He does now,' a stern voice said from behind,

and J. L. King himself strode towards the group. No one had heard the sound of a car engine pulling up in the yard. 'I heard what he said and I don't like it, not the least little bit.'

Spencer's eyes narrowed and his face took on a shifty look. 'You never asked any questions,' he muttered to his boss. 'And you were always happy with the results.'

'Until now.' Mr King stood face to face with Spencer. 'You didn't dare tie them up that tight or sack them out when I was around. You had to sneak behind my back to do it. But you're right – I should've kept a closer eye on the way you worked.'

'So what now?' Spencer squared up to Mr King, challenging him to make the next move. 'Are you gonna fire me for doing what every cowboy in

America did for over a hundred years?'

There was a long silence before J. L. King pulled a piece of folded paper out of his vest pocket. 'No,' he said, waving the paper in front of Spencer's face. 'The reason I'm gonna fire you is because you forged a breeding history for the sorrel mare we bought from the Allens. And I'm holding the proof in my hands right here, right now!'

In the round pen at Black Pearl Ranch, Allyson and Brooke were hard at work on join-up with Snowstorm and Corporal Jack, the two new ponies. Popcorn the kitten lay curled up on his favourite fence post, watching sleepily in the midday sun.

'Good job, Brooke – snake the rope along just

behind Snowstorm's back legs – drive her forward – good!' Hearing Jacob drive the truck into the yard, Allyson stopped and waved.

Keira hardly waited for her dad to park before she sprang from the truck and raced to the pen. 'Mom, Brooke – great news!' she yelled.

Allyson and Brooke left their work and came to the fence. 'What did you find out at Manning Junction?' Brooke wanted to know.

'Spencer Brown was the one who forged Miss Molly's papers!' Keira cried. 'He sold her to the Hearnes behind Mr King's back!'

'Who's Spencer Brown?'

'A guy who works – *worked* – for Mr King. He broke the law. Miss Molly didn't belong to him but he still sold her!' Keira spoke breathlessly, stumbling over some of her words. She'd been storing up the good news ever since she and her dad had left Manning Junction and now it came tumbling out.

'So the Hearnes never really owned Miss Molly?' Allyson asked slowly.

'No. She still belongs to Mr King.'

'Who, it turns out, is a good guy,' Jacob told her. 'When he found out every lousy thing that Brown had done, he called the cops.'

'Why, what else did he do wrong?' Brooke climbed the fence and swung herself down beside Keira.

'He was cruel to the ponies – he spooked them and scared them till they were broken and beaten. That's what happened to Miss Molly when Mr

King first had her as a two-year-old – Brown tried to force her into the trailer so he could truck her out to the Allens in Elk Springs.'

'Speaking of which,' Jacob interrupted. He pointed to a grey truck which had followed him down the hill. 'Jon King was happy to let me make a phone call from his place.'

'Who's this?' Brooke wondered.

'Wait and see!' Keira cried, dashing into the barn before Brooke could ask more questions.

'Hey Miss Molly!' Keira called softly as she ran down the aisle. 'How are you doing?'

The pony heard her voice and came to her stall door with wisps of straw in her mane and still the sad look on her face.

'Let's pretty you up,' Keira murmured, picking

out the straw and pushing her mane from her face. 'You need to look good. I want you to come out and meet some people.'

At this, Miss Molly pricked up her ears. She seemed to be listening to new voices out in the yard.

'Ready?' Keira asked. She opened the door, clipped a lead rope to Miss Molly's head collar and led her from the barn.

Out in the yard, Jacob was deep in conversation with two new visitors – a young guy in his twenties with light brown, curly hair and a similar-looking kid of twelve or thirteen who might be his younger brother. The boy heard Miss Molly's hooves on the gravel and, when he turned and saw her, his eyes lit up.

'It's you!' the kid said, coming to meet Keira and

Miss Molly. 'Brown Velvet – it's really you!'

Jay Allen said he'd always loved his little sorrel mare, right from the start. 'I was ten years old when Luke bought her for me,' he told Keira and Brooke. 'I woke up one morning, looked out into the corral and there she was – my perfect pony. I couldn't believe it – I thought my dream had come true!'

'Then the dream turned into a nightmare,' Luke explained. 'We found the pony had a big issue with loading into a trailer. We worked and worked with her, but we never solved the problem.'

'So we had to sell her back to Mr King,' Jay sighed.

'There's no room on a ranch for a pony with loading problems.' Luke turned to Jacob. 'I'm finding it hard to believe that you found a way around the issue, like you said on the phone.'

'Go ahead, show them,' Jacob said to Keira with a smile. He pointed to the trailer parked by the fence.

'Hold it. This might not work.' Luke warned Jay not to get up his hopes.

'You just watch!' Brooke promised. 'Go, Keira. Go, Miss Molly!'

Keira took a deep breath. *We've got to do this!* she thought. *Everything – your whole future – depends on getting this right!*

Miss Molly seemed to understand. As Keira put gentle pressure on the rope to lead her forward, she stepped out willingly.

'Cool!' Keira breathed. 'Red Star showed you how to do this, remember.'

Miss Molly listened and drew courage from Keira's voice. On she walked into the long afternoon shadow cast by the trailer, where she hesitated for a heartbeat.

'Walk on!' Keira murmured.

Miss Molly arched her neck, her ears flicked forward. Then she went straight up the ramp and out of sight.

Outside in the yard, the onlookers burst into applause.

'Good job!' Inside the dark trailer Keira breathed into Miss Molly's ear. 'You're one totally incredible, gorgeous girl!'

Jay and Luke Allen had never really wanted to let

Miss Molly go and now that they knew she was over her trailer issue they were eager to have her back. They promised they would bring their own trailer to Black Pearl Ranch the next morning and drive her home to their ranch out at Elk Springs. Mr Hearne had confirmed he was happy to let her go for free.

As for Jon King, he regretted that he'd ever set eyes on Spencer Brown and was sorry for the damage his employee had done to the Manning Junction ponies behind his back. Karl Hamlin had been ready to step into Brown's shoes as the main horse trainer there. 'No more sacking out,' Karl had promised Keira. 'From now on we use only gentle methods to school our horses, just like your dad.'

'So, it works out well,' Allyson agreed after the

Allens had left and Miss Molly was safe in her stall.

Keira and Brooke had just fetched Red Star and Annie in from the meadow. 'It worked out *brilliantly*!' they chimed.

Keira led Red Star towards his stall, but before he went in, he paused to peer over Miss Molly's door. He gave her a long look then tossed his head and stamped his foot.

Keira laughed. 'It's OK, Miss Molly, Red Star is only saying hi!'

Miss Molly snorted and tossed her head in return. Her brown eyes gleamed and she peered out from under her shiny mane as she came boldly to her door.

'She says hi too!' Keira put her arm around her pony's neck and gave him a big hug. 'Admit it, Red

Star, Miss Molly's the most beautiful thing you ever saw and you'll be sorry to see her go!'

Keira's home is **Black Pearl Ranch**, where she helps
train ponies – and lives the dream …

Black Pearl Ponies

Red Star is the love
of Keira's life and
the best pony ever.
But he's in danger:
he's gone missing
in the snowy
mountains, home
to bears and
coyotes.

Has he escaped?
Or has he been stolen?
Either way, can Keira
rescue her beloved pony in time?

Keira's home is **Black Pearl Ranch**, where she helps train ponies – and lives the dream ...

Black Pearl Ponies

Reed Walters' new pony, **Wildflower**, is beautiful but untrained. Keira warns Reed not to push her too hard, but he insists on showing her off at the local rodeo.

Disaster strikes: Wildflower bolts from the arena. Keira and her sister head off into a snowstorm to find her, forgetting the one golden rule – always stick together ...

2

Black Pearl Ponies

Black Pearl Ponies

WILDFLOWER

WILDFLOWER

JENNY OLDFIELD